For Claire
on her 9th birthday
With love from
Tia Risa

LOST PONY

GEORGE MENDOZA

Photographs by René Burri

Lost Pony

SAN FRANCISCO BOOK COMPANY, INC. San Francisco 1976

Printed in the United States of America.

Library of Congress Cataloging in Publication Data

Mendoza, George.
    Lost pony.

    Summary: Text and photos unfold the wanderings of an
orphan boy on the streets of Paris as he dreams of owning
a horse.
    [1. Orphans—Fiction   2. Paris—Fiction
3. Horses—Fiction]   I. Burri, René.   II. Title.
PZ7.M5255Lo   [Fic]   76-10274
ISBN 0-913374-43-1
ISBN 0-913374-44-X pbk.

Simon and Schuster Order Number 22348 (cloth); 22349 (paper)

Trade distribution by Simon and Schuster
A Gulf + Western Company

10 9 8 7 6 5 4 3 2 1

For Ryan and Raindrop
where it all began
and with special thanks to
Anita and Ernest Scott
who gently touched the dream

We actually live, today,
in our dreams of yesterday;
and in living those dreams we dream again.

Charles Augustus Lindbergh

At this precise moment,
as you are gazing out your window
or sitting in your chair thinking
about all the lost things out
there in the world that you
hoped and wished for, you
might let a story as frail
and real as your own life touch
the darkening time of your mind.
And if you can dream
dream for what is beyond . . .
if you can dream
dream deep
as the dream in the eyes
of the bird with the long feathers . . .

One day a young boy appeared on the streets of Paris. He had no mother or father, and it seemed as though he had no one in the world to be responsible for him. To the romantic eye he looked like a sparrow, frail and vulnerable. But through the hard eye of reality one saw a boy, poor with crumpled, soiled clothing.

If he were to walk up to you suddenly on the street, with his nine years or so of life branching out of his sapling frame, you would sense your heart going out to him. For he would make you feel as though he were that long ago, spirit-free missing in you.

If you looked closer still into his searching eyes, you would see that they turned inward away from the world, and you would find yourself being drawn back into your own secret time of innocence.

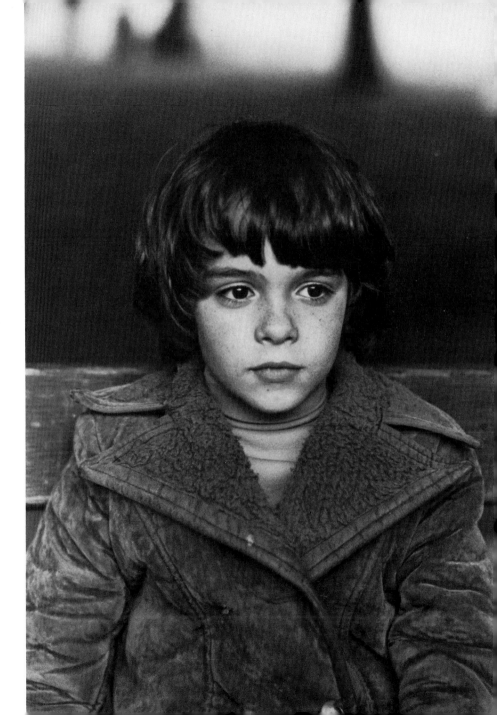

When the pâtisserie opened its shutters to begin the business of the day, the boy was first among customers to greet Monsieur Jobert.

"Bonjour, monsieur, if you please I would like some bread," said the boy as he dug deep into his corduroy pants.

When he opened his hand, Monsieur Jobert
saw a tiny colored stone. Strangely disarmed
by the boy's innocence, he took the stone and
held it up to the morning light.

"This is indeed a beautiful stone," exclaimed Monsieur Jobert.

"I polished it, sir," replied the boy with pride.

"I can see that," said Monsieur Jobert. "Now let me see what I have for you."

Turning to his baker's rack, Monsieur Jobert picked up a warm baguette of bread.

"And I baked this. . . ."

With his baguette tucked snugly under his arm, the boy wandered along the narrow,
twisting streets of Paris without a care in his head for where he
was going. Looking up into the sky of pink and blue furrows, the boy sensed the wonder of an
unexpected settlement of Spring birds swooping and chattering and circling above him everywhere.
And though he was hungry and tired, he felt as alive as the morning coming awake.

He had been in Paris once before, but that was only passing through, and then, he recalled sadly, it was in a large buslike van and he had been packed in with a lot of other lost and homeless boys who had nothing in the world except what meager possessions they were carrying in their pockets.

All the pauper boy owned was a postcard of a boy with a pony, and he treasured his possession of that postcard more than the clothes on his back or the shoes on his feet. But he didn't want to think about that time now. Not on this day when the world was opening to him and he was free.

Now, as he glided happily along through the timeless webs of streets, he waved to the sweeper and he smelled a bunch of fresh flowers from an old vendor's stall and he was overwhelmed by the living snails and giant crabs and curled up langoustines that filled a Rue Mouffetard poissonnerie.

And all who saw him could not help but stop what they were doing to take a moment
to nod or smile or talk to him.
Most of all, the boy struck wonder in them as if the spirit-clock of the day was waiting
to be set with the windings of his heart.

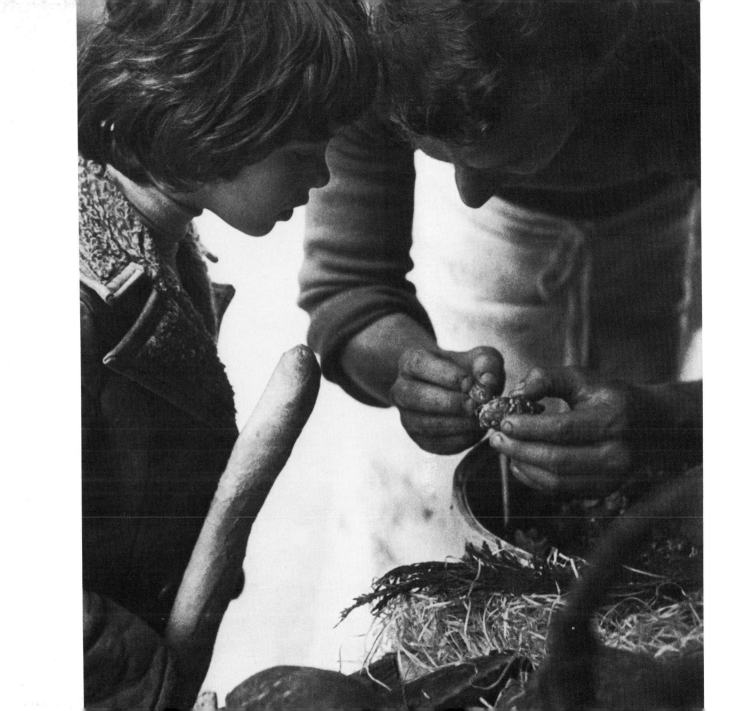

Jabs of hunger reminded him that he hadn't taken a bite since dawn. And he remembered how he had been roused furiously from his baggage room slumbers by a burly hotel porter.

But he wanted to save his bread to eat in a park, somewhere among the gardens, to share what he had with the birds or any other creature who happened to be hungry.

As he neared a bridge crossing the Seine, he was overcome by the bronze might of a horse that seemed to be lifting from its foundation into the sky. He stopped and looked up at the horse, his heart racing wildly.

The horse was enormous, as powerful as the God-like figure riding it.
Rearing his head back, the boy suddenly whinnied and snorted as though he had struck
an eternal communion with the bronze horse.
Then, pretending he was the rider holding the reins, he closed his eyes until he could
feel himself galloping over the rooftops and towers of Paris, charging into the clouds.

To have a horse! To have a horse like a God from an ancient time! To ride into the sky with silver, flashing spurs!

And now, if you have ever had a dream, you know that the dream of the boy was not to eat more or sleep secure in his own bed under a quilt a mother's hands had made for him or play ball in the park with a father who loved him or to know where he had come from or wonder where he was going.

The only dream
he had was to
have his own horse
like the boy
in the postcard . . .
like the rider
on the bridge!

When he reached the park, he found himself upon a bench, his body trembling, his face
slicked with the sweat of his hard gallop.
Patting his forehead, he noticed that a few fearless pigeons were already pecking into
his bread that lay on the bench beside him.

"Excuse me, my little friends," the boy said, still gasping for breath. "Shall we share . . . our breakfast . . . together?"
Reaching out his hand, he broke off a chunk of bread and swept it into his mouth.

"I've captured you!" boomed a voice behind the boy. Turning quickly with fear, the boy saw a man, as lean as a tube, wearing a plum velvet hat with a string denim shirt and fancy silver-tipped cowboy boots. And in front of his face he held a camera pointed at the boy that he kept clicking constantly.

"Who are you?" asked the boy as he looked
into the eye of the camera while the stranger
went on clicking and clicking.

"An artist!" replied the man. "And oh—how I have captured you . . . galloping across that bridge like a wild pony . . . well, I must say, pure art!"

"Don't you ever put your camera down?" asked the boy, amused by the artist's manner of expression as he knelt and clicked, focused and refocused, moved in close, then stepped far back, never once removing the camera from his face.

"Rather see life this way through my camera . . . more meaningful," stated the artist. "Tried to see it the other way once, but it was too real, couldn't take it all in. Now I live only to see through my camera, create only through my camera!" "You must stop sometime," said the boy. "To sleep, to eat, at least to change your film!"

"Don't sleep, don't trust food, never change film!" answered the artist. The boy tried not to laugh at the artist. He didn't want to hurt his feelings. "If you don't change film—then how can you take any pictures?" "Is that so important?" exclaimed the artist. "Besides, too mechanical to keep opening the camera, inserting film, winding up and all that, got to keep catching the light, no time for unimportant matters, no time for anything but to see and to shoot, to go on clicking and clicking."

"That's sad," said the boy quietly. "You keep everything just for yourself. You don't share your feelings with anyone. . . ."
"Exactly—you see my point!" cried the artist as he began to move his camera closer to the boy.

"Let me teach you something of life: too many people in the world believe they are artists. They paint, sculpt, write, compose, direct films, act, dabble and diddle, but I'm afraid they are overwrought with their self-importance, driven by some need to identify —when really they should be doing other more important things like—galloping across bridges!" And the artist roared with hysterical delight.

Suddenly, all the birds in the park seemed to flutter all at once around the boy's head.

"You're scaring the birds . . . ," said the boy.
"Magnificent!" shouted the artist, now jumping up and down while he clicked away.
"You should see what I see through my camera! Your head is a carousel of
feathers . . . oh, oh! This will be my most perfect work. I'll call it . . .
the bird with the long feathers. I'll make you famous by
that name, more famous than the Mona Lisa!"

And the artist went dashing off across the park with his camera masking his face,
screaming into the sky like a lunatic . . .
"The bird with the long feathers . . . the bird with the long feathers!"
The boy looked after the artist until he had finally disappeared. And he thought about
his new name and liked it very much.

Toward noon the bird with the long feathers strolled across the Jardin des Tuileries
and found himself among the open bookstalls on the street. He had never seen art
books before, and when he opened one, he was surprised
to find it filled with horses. For the longest time he looked at the book,
his imagination stirring with wonder and delight.

Walking on, he came to a museum called the Jeu de Paume. Roaming from one room to the next, he was greatly moved by each painting he saw, and it made him think about the artist he had met in the park, and he wondered what works would be hanging in the Jeu de Paume if all artists kept their feelings locked up inside themselves.

When the bird with the long feathers saw Degas' bronze horses inside the glass case
he ran up to them as though he were going to leap upon the little horses.
And once again he began to whinny and snort, his feet striking the floor hard, and
then suddenly he raced round the horses until he could feel the wind blowing through
his mane and the sound of a thousand horses was thundering beside him.

"STOP IT! STOP IT!" snapped an angry guard as he grabbed the bird with the long feathers by his collar and led him to an exit door.

"Bad boy!" grunted the guard. "You should be in school learning how to better yourself!"

"I was only pretending to be the horses in the glass case!"
said the bird with the long feathers.
"Pretend to be somewhere else!" cried the guard. "A museum is a place to be quiet, to
dream . . . what do you think the Jeu de Paume is—a rodeo?"
And the guard ushered the bird with the long feathers out the door cautioning him
finally to come back only when he could behave like a grownup, not a horse.

Reflecting upon his bruised feelings, the boy thought about his first day in the city.
There seemed to be so many different kinds of people
living close together like Monsieur Jobert and the philosopher-artist,
and there was the flower man and the street sweeper and the museum guard who
had little patience for a boy dreaming he was a horse.

So many different kinds of people and no one the same. "That's good!" said the boy aloud.

For where he had come from everything was the same; the clothes, the walls, the mornings, and the nights that never changed.

It was early afternoon, but the boy had still more dream-paths to cross:
At the carousel in the park, he watched outside a wire fence while children went
round and round laughing into the sky as their toy-colored horses bobbed up and
down, up and down, with the soft sounds of tinkling music filling the air.
And mothers and fathers stood looking at their children with love in their eyes that
promised still one more ride.

He watched some workers while they carefully assembled an old carousel of gleaming white horses, and they

accepted his offering of help for mounting the last horse in place.

And when he came across the horse that lived in the tree, they had a long conversation about all the different kinds of horses there were in the world, and the boy showed his new friend the postcard that he always carried with him.

Before they said goodbye, the boy sang a song
for the horse who lived in the tree:

"We're going to
ride together . . .
along a river bank
till we come to a
bridge that goes
to a pretty white house . . .
and we'll live there
forever,
forever and forever . . ."

High up in the sky on top of the Grand Palais, the boy saw horses leaping into the sky
and he began to gallop to the drumbeat of his dream:

Riding in the sky
riding far away . . .
give my heart
to you I say . . .
as I ride, ride
the sky today . . .

So moved was he to discover a horse in the middle of Place des Victoires that he spun round and round until his feet could feel the sky beneath, and his hands became birds, and all the cobblestones were clouds to cross . . .

When he found a discarded couronne du Roi, he placed it on his head and galloped and galloped until he reached his kingdom.

Then looking up through the trees he saw mighty Charlemagne on his gigantic horse, and he rode with Charlemagne to battle!

Coming upon Jeanne d'Arc
gleaming on her stallion,
he heard close by a guitar plucking
and a young girl's song:

"Not for flaming bronze
you set your dream,
but to ride the golden airs . . .
Jeanne d'Arc, Jeanne d'Arc,
Do I know who you are
when you cloppety-clop
down the ghostly streets of my heart . . . ?"

Oh to have a horse like that soldier,
dreamed the boy! To charge through the
smoke and cannon fire, to have a horse as
brave as his rider's heart!
And the boy galloped, galloped away, and
his dream made him taller than the world. . . .

Finally along Saint-Honoré he saw an extraordinary stuffed pony standing inside an expensive toy store. The pony had big dark eyes and soft black hair with a fluffy white mane falling over its neck and eyes.

A small tag on the pony said it had been made in Spain.

The boy stood wondering how it would feel to sit high on the pony's back.

What a gift to receive, he thought. To have a pony like that—and then he remembered his pony, and taking out the postcard he looked down at it and wished . . .

O to have a horse like a farmboy,
only a pony, a pony,
to feed and love forever . . .

That evening before dark the boy had still one more dream.

He had gone back to the old carousel of gleaming white horses that now sat quietly alone.

Lifting himself up upon a horse that was saddled with a red and blue blanket and golden tassels, he imagined his horse slowly beginning to move under him, and suddenly they seemed to be going round and round, up and down, faster and faster, and music carouseled everywhere in the air and on and on he rode into his dreams.

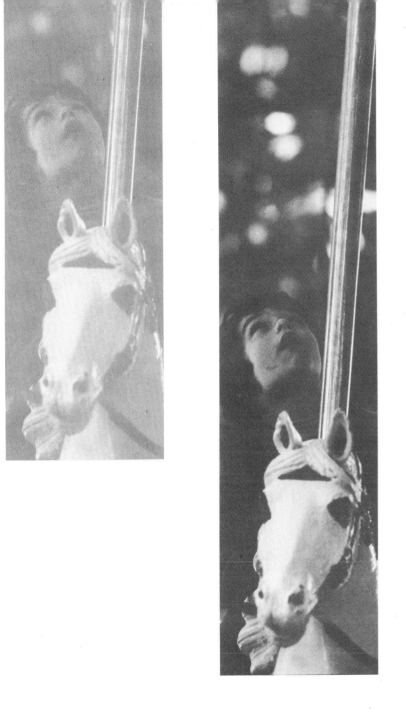

And then he felt someone gently tugging at him trying to wake him up and he thought he saw Mother Superior from the orphanage close to him whispering into his ear, "Come, Stephan, the ride is over . . . it's time to go home. . . ."

And when he got down from the horse and took her hand, something fell out of his pocket, but he was too tired to look back to see what it was he had left behind.